Embarrassing Dad by Chris Allton

For the best dad of all

My Dad

Chapter 1 - My Dad

My dad is so embarrassing. I mean ... really embarrassing! From as early as I can remember he always did everything he could to embarrass me. You won't believe the things he has done, or worst still, made me do. How can I explain? How can I put it into words, so you get an accurate idea? Your dad may be embarrassing but not on the scale that mine is. It's like he has a PhD in it. Dr Embarrass, a master of making fun, an A star in annoying. Where do I start?

Dad is in his forties, but he acts like he is in his thirties or even twenties at times. He is going slightly bald (though he will never admit it) and he combs his hair back with wax to cover his shiny head. He wears thick-rimmed glasses that make him look like Clark Kent (but not Superman!)

He has a beard which I used to think was really embarrassing, but I got used to it the longer it got until one day... yes, you're right...

he cut it off. Now he has a short beard which he moans about as secretly I know he wishes he'd kept it long. It serves him right for getting drunk in the pub and getting one of his friends to "trim" it for him.

He is not overly tall, but not short. Just average. He has a little bit of a tummy on him which is cute and cuddly, but he keeps saying he will lose it when he does some exercise. He always wears a shirt and tie for work or, out of work, a checked shirt, jeans and brown cowboy boots. He thinks he is so cool! If he ever does wear a t-shirt or, heaven forbid, a pair of shorts, he looks so, so strange.

That goes some way to explain how he is embarrassing because of the way he looks but it is the things he does that make it even worse. I like lists, and I love making lists in lists. You'll see what I mean. Let me start with the top five examples so far in my life of how embarrassing my dad is.

1. When I was younger, between the ages of five and eleven, I went to a lot of parties. You know what I mean. While at primary school, children go to lots of parties all the time. You all remember the parties at soft play areas, or

bowling, or going for a pizza. Times after school, or at weekends, when you spent great times with your friends. Being locked in a room, stuck in a ball pool and being fed on cheese sandwiches, cake and sweets. However, in my case, there was always one added accessory. Dad would always come to the party with me. My mum did this, but she usually talked to the other mums.

Dad would come in, wave at the other parents and then jump in the ball pool, climb up the soft play area, or push me out of the way when it came to food time. No matter how many times I asked him to go, he would always stand around trying to look cool. He thought he was John Travolta from Saturday Night Fever or someone from Strictly Come Dancing. And if it was karaoke, it was even worse. He would always get up and sing a song by Elvis Presley called Suspicious Minds.

If your dad singing at one of your school friend's party wasn't bad enough, then you should have seen his preparation. He would disappear to the toilets with a little black leather bag, and he told me that while he was in there, he would be applying wax to his hair to slick it back with a comb and some horrible smelling aftershave that made him smell like a grandad.

This got worse if it was in a social centre, pub or restaurant. Somewhere where there was a bar selling alcohol. Don't get me wrong, Dad didn't get drunk, but he may as well have done. He used to stand at the bar with one hand holding the bar rail, the other stretched outright, and he proceeded to warm up for his dance or vocal routine. There he was, a bearded, slightly balding gentleman, performing a full Plié to name one of the many ballet moves he attempted.

2. In the supermarket, he is so embarrassing. He walks up and down the aisles shouting things out about me so people can hear. And he does it at the most inappropriate times. Here are the top three moments in the supermarket:

a) Standing at the checkout and talking to the check-out person as if they were his best friend. Then saying something "funny" like, "I've got your favourite cat food, you know the rotten fish flavour you really like, but we are going to have to get you a new toothbrush as your breath stinks." He just laughs and thinks he is hysterical. Why, oh why does he do this?

b) Going to the underwear department and holding bras up in front of him and asking my opinion. He does this every time, and he thinks it is hilarious, but of course, I don't know what to do with myself. I just walk off at times as he is so embarrassing

c) Shouting down busy aisles - really loud. Dad would send me to go and get some milk or bread; then, he will stand at the other end of the aisle and just shout random things at me from a distance. For example (I told you I like lists in lists):

i) He would send me for milk, explaining what colour carton and what size precisely. Then when I pick it up, he would shout "I said silk, not milk. Green silk!" And then to make things worse, he would start mooing very, very loud. All the old dears and shoppers around would walk away shaking their heads, and I would do the walk of shame to the trolley.

ii) Down the personal hygiene aisle, Dad starts spraying deodorant, or shaving foam and then rubbing it in my face. One time he missed under his arm and sprayed a lady in the face causing her to cough and splutter rushing outside for fresh air.

iii) In the frozen section, whenever I look at what ice cream or ice lollies I want, Dad always picks me up and threatens to throw me in the freezers, squashing choc ices and other such delights. His actions mean no one comes near us. He is so, so embarrassing

3. Back to the main list. This takes us to our trips to the swimming pool. Dad has never been an excellent swimmer, but I love it. I go to swimming training three times a week and to be honest; I'm pretty good at it. Dad, on the other hand, is like a stone. He just sinks. He doesn't like swimming, I know that, but he comes with me as he knows I love it.

This all sounds nice so how can it be embarrassing. Well, other than the fact that Dad always complained about me not being able to swim in the "swimmers" lane as I was a child (he would get out and argue with the lifeguard that I was a much better swimmer than him and that if she needed to jump in and save anyone it would be him not me), the worst was still to some.

We had a swimming party for my birthday when I was nine. Inflatable, water squirting everywhere, you get the idea. But as the session finished and it was time to get out, my dad was the last in the pool. It was bad enough that he was wearing armbands the whole time, but as he got out of the pool, his trunks remained in the water. So, what did he do? Took off the armbands and put one in front of him and one behind and continued to the changing rooms. All the old dears who were coming in for their aqua aerobics gasped and touched rubbed their swimming caps (no doubt covering a blue rinse).

When a female lifeguard approached him, and made a complaint, he merely raised his hands in surrender. I was so embarrassed, but he seemed not concerned in the slightest that he stood there completely naked holding up a pair of armbands. My friends all laughed no end. Not only then but for weeks after about my embarrassing dad. I didn't dare speak to anyone at school as that situation was always brought up.

4. Picking me up in the car. As I have got, older this has happened more and more. The more he does it, the funnier he thinks it is. Dad always tells a story of how he did this when he was younger to his friend "Haggis" so, naturally, he must do it to me too. Initially, he would pull up in the car ready to pick me up. As I go to get

the handle, he moves the car forward, and I miss it.

This continues several times as my friends are usually watching. If I refuse to move, he would wind down the window and tell me he was sorry and tell me to get in, but... guess what... he would then move on again.

One time I got so angry with him I clung to the door through the open window. A lady came to ask if I was ok, and I smiled at her but as I did, Dad stood on the accelerator and set off down the street with me holding onto the door frame. I started running first, but then as he got quicker and quicker, I clung on for dear life and lifted my legs. Eventually, slowed down, leant over and pulled me into the car headfirst. Mum would have gone mad if she'd known he'd done that. (As embarrassing as it was, it was actually quite cool, but I won't tell Dad that).

5. The band! One of the most embarrassing things about my dad is his band. He plays double bass in a rock and roll band with some silly name. If it's not bad enough that he is a band, he also wears a stupid shirt and sunglasses every time he plays. He and his friends all wear the same clothes: a black fifties shirt with a white

trim and silly symbols on it; a blue suit with a little black handkerchief sticking out of the top pocket; sunglasses even when they are inside and, to top it all off, a pair of silly shoes that gangsters used to wear in the 1920's. He and his friends think they look so cool, but they look stupid. Embarrassing moments when my dad plays in his band:

a) On the few occasions, I have been dragged along to watch him, he will say something embarrassing from the stage. For example, "That little girl over there is my daughter, would you like to come up here on stage and say hello to everyone?" I would always shake my head and bury it in my hands.

b) His friends are as equally weird as him. Whether it be the ones who are in this band or the ones he hangs around with at other times. They are just odd. My dad says most people are weirdos, but I always correct him and say he is the weirdo.

c) The worst time was when he turned up for parents evening dressed up in all his band clothes because he was going to a gig after. I made him keep his coat on, but he kept getting out the sunglasses and pretending he was a famous rock star or something. My friends kept going on about it, but I hated it. He was so, so embarrassing.

So, as you can see, my dad is very, very, VERY embarrassing. I'm sure he does all these things to make my life miserable, and so he can laugh about them with his friends. I love him, but I just wish he would chill out and be a bit normal at times.

Chapter 2 - My Mum

I love spending time with Dad. He and my mum don't live together anymore. They separated and got divorced when I was small. It's not a problem though as it is just normal life for me now. Half the week, I'm with Dad, the other half with my mum. She is embarrassing at times (like most other parents I assume) but not to the level of Dad.

The main thing you need to know about my mum is that she is a member of Ladies First. If you are wondering what Ladies First is, it's a bit like the Women's Institute but with a slight difference. It was formed by my mum (and some of her friends), so it is apparently "better". It's a group where women get together and talk about things and do activities to help them as a group.

If you ask Dad about it, he jokes that they are plotting the end of all men, especially him. He says that if a lot of mums get together, it can only mean trouble for dads. Of course, he is just joking - being embarrassing again! From what my mum tells me they do lots of things like the Women's Institute do.

They have meetings, make quilts, have lessons on how to use things like digital cameras and protest about things like the poor treatment of bees and how if they become extinct life on Earth will end. She will often make cakes. Lemon drizzle cake is the best. We call it "The Drizzler". That is delicious: it is so addictive. I do quite a bit of baking at home, and I have tried to make "The Drizzler", but it always seems like it is missing a secret ingredient. My mum says that when I am old enough, and I join Ladies First, I will get the secret recipe and will be able to make it myself.

The other type of cake she has made was a fruitcake. This was done with her friend, Carol: they spent a long time perfecting the ingredients, having tasting sessions with other members; meetings about decorations and shape due to the form it was going to take and how and when the final masterpiece would be created. The plan was to create a cake for the Prime Minister of the country - Mrs Smith.

She was the honorary member of Ladies First (this meant she wasn't a member, but my mum really wanted her to be one). They planned to create a cake so fantastic that the Prime Minister would ask to join Ladies First, leading to all women in the country entering the ranks and that would make my mum feel even more important. The final ingredients for the cake were agreed (lemon drizzle cake); it was just the shape that needed finalising. These were the top three options for the cake shape:

i) Big Ben and the Houses of Parliament

ii) Great Britain

iii) The Prime Minister's head

My favourite was number three, but I don't think my mum agreed.

"It would be too complicated. Imagine trying to balance a cake head on a tiny neck. It would just collapse."

"I'm sure you'd be able to manage it, Mum," I replied positively.

"It has to be perfect. The Prime Minister will never join our group if her head falls off a cake!" came the reply. I smiled weakly in response, unsure of what to say next.

Meetings for Ladies First took place at either my mum's house or down the road at the local cocktail bar called Lee's Bar. This venue had very old-fashioned, pink neon lights at the front - Lee's Bar spelt out, sizzling day and night like an electric flycatcher in a busy kitchen.

My mum and Carol were always there, discussing Ladies First and other such plans but mainly to drink gin and tonic. You know the sort: colossal fishbowl glasses with lots of ice; a selection of fruit from the dining table, cucumber from the fridge or some herbs from the garden. They both thought they were very sophisticated because they drank "posh" drinks.

While there, Carol, who was a similar age to my mum (forty-something) flirted with Lee, the owner of the bar. She would sit at the bar twiddling her hair between her fingers smiling at Lee. He always looked smart with a black flat-cap, black polo shirt and designer stubble. My mum disapproved and often told me of her disappointment in Carol the next time she saw me after their meetings.

"I don't know what she's playing at. She is meant to be a top member of Ladies First, not some soppy teenager - no offence meant dear."

"None took," I sighed in reply. "So, what other plans have you come up with?"

"Well dear," she continued. "I have organised a special evening for us. It is going to be our annual social event with lots of members coming, so I have to make a good impression." I always thought that this was some booze club for members as a lot of the ladies got a little tipsy, except my Mum. She was always very sensible and kept to the strict agenda of the meetings (which she wrote) and one glass of gin and slim line tonic.

"Anything else?" I quizzed.

"Well as you know, we have a guest speaker at these meetings, so we have a secret, surprise visitor for next month's meeting."

"Who is it?" I enquired.

"If I told you it wouldn't be a secret would it. However, you will see as you will be there. Time for you to become a junior member of Ladies First."

"When is the meeting?"

"Three weeks on Saturday," came the reply. My heart sank.

"But I'm at dad's house that night. We have a special surprise planned."

"Well, this is far more important than anything you might do with THAT man."

"That man," I replied, "is my dad and we have made plans."

"Well, you will just have to change them then, won't you."

My mum always went on about me joining Ladies First. She said when I was older it would be perfect as we would both be members and we could run the group. Not quite my idea of perfection. My mum is a bit of a control freak. Let me explain:

1) A TV in my room. At Dad's house, I have a small TV in my room. I can escape and chill out there, catching up on some series, doing some drawing or just relaxing. At my mum's there is no such thing as I think she thinks the television is the devil in my room and will lead me astray. I won't do homework; I won't tidy my underwear from the floor, I won't go to sleep. You get the idea. She wants me to watch the TV with her, but it is always what she wants to watch - dancing programmes or baking competitions. In contrast, Dad will always watch what I want when we both watching together. He misses out on football and his embarrassing music videos and

20

watches all the programmes I like. No matter how many times I ask.

2) Time spent on my phone. Like the television, the phone is an evil influence. My Dad is a little paranoid about this, thinking that I am texting boys (as if I'd tell him if I was) but my mum believes that it is eating away at my brain and sucking my soul out of me. Dad understands (he's on his all the time too).

3) Controlling my friends. I have lots of friends at school and some friends near where I live. However, my mum encourages me to be friends with certain children as she is friends with their parents. It's like she wants to set up a parent and child friend-circle. Some of them are great, and friends at school, but others are so, so dull, and I would never be friends with them in a million years, but I am "persuaded" to do so.

Who is the child? If my mum and I argue (or shall I say, I disagree with her and she puts me right), then often, she will sulk and complain about my behaviour. I'm the one who ends up apologising just to get her out of a mood. I'm sure sometimes she would stomp off to her room given half a chance.

I decided to disappear into my room and text Dad to tell him what my mum had said. She was busy downstairs, making a quilt or crocheting. Some stereotypical activity of the Ladies group. I got the reply I expected from Dad. Unsurprisingly, he was not so happy and made some comment about my mum's agenda and that he was going to sort her out. He always said stuff like this, and it made me smile. This was his reply:

"I will text her and sort this out if you want. She is probably busy watching Mamma Mia again, or trying to work out how to use the DVD control so she can watch Mamma Mia again! Anyway, let me know what you want to do and if you want me to text. I love you xxx."

Dad texts me every day. He moans that I never reply (I am busy and do have a life you know) but I do like reading his texts. I know he is there and I know he loves me.

Chapter 3 – School

I feel safe at school - away from them both. Dad being embarrassing and Mum being bossy. At school, I escape the bickering, the irrational behaviour and the control. I seem to be able to focus on me for six and a half hours in a day. My teacher, Mr Byrne, is a very understanding teacher.

He understands my situation and that my parents are divorced. He's great because he knows which mornings I've come from my mum's and which I've come from Dad's. Everything is a bit last minute with Dad. To be honest, it's not his fault, it's usually mine, but he does allow me longer in bed. With my mum, everything is to a set time, an established routine. Military style!

I go to a school called St. Mary's Primary School. It's a great school, and I love it. It has all the vital things for as primary school: a great playground, with a tyre trail, goal posts to keep the boys interested; a tuck shop on a Friday break time, where crisps and sweets are sold, but more importantly, Mrs Gaskell (the school cook) sells her flapjack. This is the best: it is to die for.

We also have a dance club on a Thursday dinner time, but this is freestyle dance to the tunes we pick from the internet, courtesy of Mrs Aspinall, the Year 2 teacher. She's a bit of a dragon at times, but a great teacher and she lets us dance our dinner times away. All the staff are friendly, apart from one. Let me explain. Here are the teachers in my school. Let's see if they match any of the staff you may have in yours.

Reception - Miss Gallagher - She always has a cup of tea in her hand and never actually seems to do any work at all. She seems to stand around and talk to the other teaching assistants in the room (Miss Hogg and Mrs Westall).

Year 1 - Mr Spencer - He is so lovely and kind and all the children in Year One think he is fantastic. He wears silly Christmas jumpers from December 1st every year: some that a have lights flashing on them, some that are musical, some that are both, but he wears a Christmas jumper every day.

Year 2 - Mrs Aspinall - Strict but fair. She has a castle built in the corner of her room for the reading corner and her displays are always perfect.

Year 3 - Miss Howell - She is the exception to the rule. She is so very fierce and takes no messing from the children, or the other staff. She continually argues with Mr Byrne, calling him lazy and that he never does anything correctly. We are quiet when the Headteacher comes into the classroom, but we daren't breathe when Miss Howell is on the prowl.

Year 4 - Mr Hargreaves - He is very tall, and some of the children (and parents) call him BFG as he is so tall and so kind.

Year 5 - Mr Sansom - He is the untidiest, most disorganised teacher in the school. He is always late for assemblies, and his desk looks like a bomb has been dropped on it. He is also the sporty teacher, so he wears shorts all year round.

Year 6 - Mr Byrne - You know about him, he's my class teacher.

Headteacher - Mr McKevitt - He is the boss. You don't really see him unless he is walking around the classrooms, taking assembly or… you're in trouble. Miss Howell often sends children to him when she has shouted at them. People used to think that he would yell at them even more but as we got older in school, we found it was more a case of making children feel happy so they would go back to Miss Howell's class. He even had a box of exclusive chocolate bars he would give to children who visited him.

You may not believe this, but my embarrassing dad and controlling mum are both teachers as well. This, in itself, is a bit of a nightmare. Let me explain. Imagine getting homework from school and then your parents asking about it. No, not just -

"Have you done your homework?" but "Is this homework at the correct level for you?" It goes on... "I wonder if this is pushing you enough?" or "I wouldn't set homework like this in my class!" As I said, thankfully this all happens at home, not at school. I can just be ordinary at school, not stand out or be a pawn in the middle of an argument.

In my class, which is the top class (Year Six), Mr Byrne makes every day great fun. We all know where we stand with him and how far we can push him before we get into trouble. He likes talking about computers and new technology, so we can manage to waste an English lesson by talking to him about new apps or tablets, and he proceeds to tell us how it will change education or our lives if we follow what he says. We do, and that means we miss an hour's lesson on semicolons or adverbial phrases. I can recommend trying it one day. Find what your teacher likes to talk about and keep them talking about it. My friends and I have a fantastic time doing this with Mr Byrne. Here are the top three times we got Mr Byrne off track and avoided lessons:

Why we should be allowed phones in class - This is a great one as he does not think it would be good for children to have phones at all, never mind in class. He says that the government use phones to track where people are and to listen in to private conversations. He said that since Mrs Smith became Prime Minister things have just gone from bad to worse. We provide arguments like we could use the internet, take pictures, send homework via text message, etc. but he says that it is too dangerous as someone could intercept your homework and change all the answers.

The benefits of using kitchen utensils in the classroom - Now this idea he is entirely behind. He thinks that by having different kitchen items around the class, the school would be much more efficient. For example:

An iron to get the creases out of scrunched up pieces of paper or when the corner of your page gets all messed up.

A dish drainer on your desk to store equipment. Where plates would go, you can slot in your books. Where spoons and forks should go, your pen, pencil and ruler can replace them.

A microwave to warm up Mr Byrne's cold cups of tea, to make hot chocolate on a winter's morning, or to heat up gloves and scarves before break time. You get the idea. Mr Byrne loved talking about these ideas.

The best music group in the world - This final one gets Mr Byrne extremely angry. He hates all modern music and listens to old stuff like The Rolling Stones or The Beatles (like Dad). He's never heard of any recent music and just complains and tells us how great his music is as it has stood the test of time and that our music will be forgotten in twelve months' time.

We have a great time in class as you can see. Mr Byrne lets us get away with all sorts if Mr McKevitt isn't doing his rounds. When the Headteacher comes in the class, we know we must be well behaved. I say that, but some of my friends don't agree. They love to take it to the next level. Here are examples of my friends pushing the limits beyond the norm:

One child in my class (Phil) once told Mr Byrne to shut up! It was obvious and the rest of the class went silent. Mr Byrne doesn't get cross very often, and he keeps calm to sort things out. As this happened, Mr McKevitt came into the classroom, and he asked what was going on. The next thing that happened involved all the children trying not to laugh. Let me explain.

Mr McKevitt started shouting at Phil, but he just looked so unimpressed. Mr McKevitt asked if Phil had anything to say. The response was something no one expected. "I have a talking cat at home," Phil answered calmly.

"What?" bellowed Mr McKevitt.

"I have a talking cat at home. It can say lots of words," Phil continued. "It says good morning and whether it is hungry or not." Mr McKevitt, on the other hand, was lost for words.

"What are you talking about? What has that got to do with this situation?"

"I'm going to go on Britain's Got Some Talent and show the world," Phil explained.

"I think you need to apologise to Mr Byrne for what you said and to me for wasting my time, don't you?"

"Well I suppose so, but soon I'll have a famous cat and so much money I can pay you to shut up!" came Phil's response. Everyone burst out laughing, including Mr Byrne. Everyone except Mr McKevitt who marched Phil straight out of the class and into his office.

2) The other memorable time again happened as Mr McKevitt came into the room. It is almost as if children wait for him to come in and involve him in the joke. Alexa, one of my friends, was talking with Mr Byrne as the Headteacher entered. She accidentally called Mr Byrne "Dad". This alone caused much hilarity but what followed was even funnier. Mr McKevitt thought it was a great joke and was laughing at Mr Byrne. Alexa was embarrassed but decided to take it one step further.

"Well it could be worse, I could have said it to you," she responded to Mr McKevitt.

"I've been called Dad plenty of times," he replied, chuckling to himself.

"I wouldn't have called you Dad," she answered, "More like Grandad!" Again, we all laughed, and Mr McKevitt left the room, as red as a tomato, lost for words. I'm sure you have called a teacher Mum or Dad in the past. I know I have. It's so embarrassing, but would you dare call your Headteacher Grandma or Grandad!

I have lots of friends at school. We all get on very well, and that is down to Mr Byrne. I've already mentioned some of the characters in my class but let me give you some more details. Here is the unofficial register (or part of it).

Phil - He's the oldest in the class but is small. He looks like he should be in the infants he's that tiny.

Alexa - She's quiet most of the time, but when she wants to have a joke, she is so funny.

Fatty - That's not his real name, that's Jason, but everyone calls him Fatty. Ironically, he is slim, and when we ask him why he is called Fatty, he says he doesn't know. So, we just call it him, affectionately.

Holly - Her dad and my dad were in a band many years ago. She suffers my music pain.

So that is school, my safe place, away from embarrassing Dad and Controlling Mum. My friends are always there for me, but with what was about to follow, I needed them more than ever. Parents evening was after school, and I had the first appointment straight after school. Mum and Dad always came and sat together to listen to how I was doing. From my classroom window, I could see them both on the playground. My mum was talking to some of the other mums, and she was looking very embarrassed. Why?

In another part of the playground was Dad. For some reason (bearing in mind it is November), he was dressed in flowery shorts, socks and sandals. He still had a shirt and tie on but was wearing his sunglasses and listening to music, through headphones on his phone. If that was not bad enough, he was also dancing. The bell rang for the end of the day, and I could see them both heading towards the door.

Chapter 4 - The Argument

"I cannot believe that you are wearing that!" my mum said as Dad danced into the classroom.

"What do you mean? I'm so cool, ain't that right?" he replied turning to me.

"Dad you are so embarrassing, I can't believe you are dressed like that. You just want to be the centre of attention."

"No I don't," he replied, "I'm just me."

"Well why don't you try being you somewhere else?" my mum retorted. Dad looked a bit upset by this. He looked at me hoping for some reassurance that everything was ok. I tried to smile weakly, but it apparently did not work. Dad looked devastated.

"I'll just sit down then shall I. Mr Byrne won't be able to see my shorts if I'm sat down."

"Thanks, Dad," I answered positively.

Mr Byrne had been to the staff room and returned to the classroom with a cup of coffee in his hand and a file under his arm. From what he could see, Dad was sat with a shirt and tie on and looked very "normal". My mum pulled up a chair next to Dad, waiting for My Byrne to take a seat. Just when I thought normality had returned, my Dad shouted out

"Yo, Byrney Boy… give me five!" Mr Byrne just looked at him then turned to my mum.

"Thanks for coming, how are you?" My mum rolled her eyes in the direction of Dad.

"Things could be better, but then again, they could be a lot, lot worse."

"I can imagine!" Mr Byrne replied. From that point on, Dad was very quiet. He never said much at Parents Evening, he never did. Except to ask if I was behaving or playing my violin still. My mum however always came with a long list of questions or statements she wanted to make, and as usual, she made her favourite comment

"Well, I am a teacher you know."

"Oh, I know," replied Mr Byrne, slightly sarcastically. Everyone in school knew my mum was a teacher, and so did all the parents. Dad, however, just sat there, quiet and listened.

"So, is she meeting her targets? Is she applying herself? Will she meet the grade?" The barrage of questions continued from my mum.

"Well, she is on target, but she does seem a little distracted in class at times. I'm not sure what is causing it. It seems like she has a lot on her mind. Is there anything happening at home that may be causing this?"

"Well, I wonder," interrupted my mum, giving Dad a dirty look.

"What's that supposed to mean?" Dad replied.

"You know full well. She is so embarrassed by you and the things you do. It's no wonder she doesn't want to come to you anymore."

"Now hang on a minute," Dad answered back, "what are you saying? You tell me what I have done wrong to upset her?"

"You mean you don't know, you really are unbelievable," came Mum's response. Mr Byrne cleared his throat, noticing the straining necks of other parents outside the classroom.

"Perhaps this is not the place for this now?"

"No, no you are quite right," my mum answered, her dragon temper calming now. I looked at Dad. The look of dejection was spreading across his face, and I could see he was genuinely worried and upset. I smiled at him and he forced one back.

Our slot at Parents Evening finished, and my mum and I stood up to leave. I looked at Dad.

"I'll wait till you've gone, so I don't embarrass you anymore."

"At least you're thinking of her now," Mum argued back, but Dad just sat there. My mum led me by the handout of the classroom, through the school door and across the playground towards her car. I felt so sorry for Dad. I had never told my mum that I didn't want to see Dad, ever. I did not understand why she said that to him, but the mood she was in I wasn't going to bring that up now.

As we crossed the hopscotch and giant 100 square in the yard, I looked back to my classroom. There was Dad, still sat at the desk, talking to Mr Byrne. They were probably discussing what had just happened as it was quite unbelievable. Then, the funniest thing happened. As I was about to turn away, Dad got up and, as he did, so did Mr Byrne. They both looked around the room, then fist bumped, then slapped hands. They looked like they were in a gang or something.

It was bizarre that Dad would do that when I was not there as he would always try and do that with me to embarrass me, yet here he was, without me, making secret handshakes with my teacher. Again, I felt now was not the appropriate time to discuss this with my mum so I got in the car, and we drove home, in silence.

A few days passed before I decided to say anything to my mum. I knew she would go mad at any mention of Dad so I thought it best to keep quiet. School carried on as normal. Mr Byrne did not mention anything about the crazy handshake he had with Dad, and I did not dare bring it up. There were a few comments from some of my friends about Dad's attire on Parents Evening but nothing out of the ordinary.

My friends all knew what Dad was like and it was accepted. Holly often said that her dad (Mick) was just as embarrassing. He used to be in a band with Dad but stopped playing and "grew up", unlike Dad! However, she said that her older sister Anna now plays the guitar and wants to be like her dad. Can you imagine?

"Your dad was nice and fashionable the other day I see," Fatty commented.

"You know what he's like Fatty, anything to embarrass me," I replied.

"And you wouldn't have it any other way," he responded. I laughed, but as I thought about it, I contemplated if I should change Dad. Would I want him any other way?

First off, the beard. When he started growing it, I complained. I begged him not to grow it, but he did, and I must admit I liked it. Then he cut it off, and I complained. Many years ago, he did the same thing, grew it long so he looked like a wizard and I moaned. Then, one afternoon, he turned up at school to pick me up with a shaven face. I walked out of class at the end of the day, looked at him and burst into tears. I don't know why I suppose it was just the change. Something new, something different. So, should he keep the beard? Yes.

The clothes he wears are smart. I suppose he looks smart, even if it is the same style of clothes day after day. He could wear things a lot worse all the time. If I could choose what he wore, I'd pick… I don't know what I'd pick. What do dad's in their forties wear? And the band he plays in, I know he does it because it is something he enjoys and he plays at weekends to earn extra money to buy me nice things.

I suppose I just wish he wouldn't embarrass me as much as he does. I need to know why he does it.

I eventually decided to speak to my mum about the dreaded incident. I had to prepare myself and her for the "mood" that would follow. This involved a series of events that had to be in place before any serious discussion could take place.

The first thing I would have to do was decide precisely what I was going to say. I would write prompt notes of the key points I needed to raise and then try and predict the responses I would get from my mum. Once these points had been decided, I would tend to practise the opening lines in front of a mirror. At times, I would decide if I need to cry when I start speaking, or do I make a joke or should I just put a serious face on. (Crying is a good one as the adult always feels sorry for you).

Picking the right time is vital. Do not start the dreaded conversation if the adult has just walked in the door after work. At times, it may be better to do it if the adult is about to leave the house as it may give them time to think alone. However, you do not want to leave the person worrying or upset all day. I often find it is best to pick a time when things are calm and quiet, arrange a meeting and then move onto the next step.

Ensure the setting is comfortable. My mum's chair is where she needs to be sat. Comfy and relaxed. Accompanying this must be a drink of some sort. The drink you choose depends on the severity of the situation. Drinks rank in this order:

a) Low-risk cases = a glass of orange or lemonade

b) Medium-risk cases = a cup of coffee or tea (potentially something with lemon, ginger or some other fancy herbs).

c) High-risk cases = gin and tonic!

Be direct and say what needs to be said. Do not skirt around the issue - say what needs to be said. Then... wait for the response.

Finally, be prepared for silence - a long silence. My mum is very good at this, and sometimes it can last hours. This is what causes the most pain (for me).

Dad, on the other hand, has an entirely different set of rules. Here are the rules for telling Dad serious news.

a) See Dad and tell him.

b) That's it!

Anyway, back to the conversation with my mum.

"Mum, why did you tell Dad that I don't want to see him anymore?" I asked tentatively.

"My dear, are you happy with the way your father behaves?"

"Well, he is a bit embarrassing, but I've never said that I don't want to see him. Did you see his face when you told him that? He looked so sad."

It is all he deserves. He is a joke, and I will not let him humiliate you anymore. You deserve so much better than him. When you join Ladies First, you will see that there are much more important things in life than your embarrassment of a father."

"But Mum, I have never said I don't want to go. He was really upset. Why did you say it?" She sighed and looked at me with the usual look she does. One that says she knows better than me and this is for my own good.

"Sometimes things happen, and you have to believe that the adults know what is best for you. Unfortunately, in this situation, your father is not acting like an adult, so I must take control.

You say you still want to see him, but I think it is best if you limit the time you spend with him. He is a bad influence, and I think that if you cut down with the time you spend with him, then he will change his tune and behave a little more maturely."

"But…"

"No sweetheart, now you listen. I have decided that you can still see him but you are not staying over and your time with him will be limited. I know you are not happy about it, but I am making these decisions for the best. For you!" I realised that it was time to sit and listen and not reply. One of those moments when you know that nothing you say will change your parent's opinion. I needed to talk to Dad.

Chapter 5 - Dad's Crazy Idea

I really wanted to see Dad, but I was unsure what to say. The last time I had seen him, he looked so sad, sat there in his flowery shorts and sandals. Now, I must go and see him, tell him I can't stay overnight and that my mum isn't happy with him - again. I got dropped off outside his house. My mum did not want to come in and speak to him or make polite chit-chat. I walked up the path to the door and nervously put my hand on the door handle. I took a great big deep breath and opened the door.

On an average day, Dad would be on his computer or playing his guitar or double bass. Today was different. He was just sat on the settee, staring at fire erupting in the log burner. No music, no television. Just sat gazing into space.

"Hiya Dad'" I called positively.

"Alright trouble," came the reply. Dad always called me trouble, as long as I could remember. Today, however, the fun seemed to be gone from his voice. "Everything ok?"

"Not really Dad. Have you spoke to Mum?"

"Yes, I have."

"Are you cross with me?"

"Cross with you? Never. I know what your mother is like. I have always taught you to be honest with me. No matter what, you can talk to me. No matter how much you think it may upset me, you must tell me what's bothering you. So, I will now give you a chance. Is there anything you want to tell me?"

"Dad, I never told Mum that I did not want to come anymore."

"Promise me; I need to know the truth from you."

"Dad, I swear. I don't know why she said that. I have asked her, and she said it is for the best and that you do nothing but embarrass me. She thinks it would be better if I didn't spend as much time with you. She thinks that, not me."

"Ok, that's what I thought." He opened his arms to hug me. "We will sort this, don't you worry. Come and sit down here, I have something to tell you." I sat down next to him, and he told me to get comfy. I felt a bit strange, as I was unsure what he was going to say to me. I never expected what he was about to say.

"Your mother is the leader of an evil secret society."

"You mean Ladies First?" I replied.

"Exactly," Dad came back straight away. "They have lost the plot."

"What do you mean?"

"Well you tell me what you know about Ladies First, and I'll tell you what I know."

"Well I know they have lots of meetings. Some, lots of women turn up to, sometimes just Mum and Carol."

"I see and what happens at these meetings?" Dad questioned.

"Well, Mum says they talk about all sorts of stuff: making quilts, learning how to use a digital camera, baking cakes. Pretty boring stuff really."

"So, have you seen these quilts being made? The camera lessons taking place? The cakes being made?"

"Well, I have seen the plans for cake making and have tasted some examples. The Drizzler is amazing." Dad raised his eyes and took a sharp intake of breath.

"So, you have seen the quilt making or digital camera lessons?"

"Yeah, well I think so. Now you have said it, I can't think of a time I saw them making a quilt. I have seen a quilt mum says they have made, but I haven't seen them make it."

"That's what I'm trying to say. Things aren't what they seem. How are your mum's photographs nowadays? Any better?" I laughed.

"Ha-ha, no not at all. She still manages to crop off people's heads or out of focus."

"And this is someone who goes to regular camera lessons." He grinned to himself but also shook his head in disbelief. "You think they are all about having talks and saving the bees but believe me they are doing a lot of things that would make you worry."

"Like what?" I asked inquisitively.

"What I tell you, you will probably not believe. All the activities they do in Ladies First is just a cover. They are a secret and very dangerous society. What you think is a craft group, I'm telling you is a group of elite trained women. They regularly visit the shooting range."

"What? The shooting range?" I exclaimed.

"I'm not joking," Dad replied, "they are a dangerous bunch. They communicate online through secret codes, untraceable by anyone." I sat there gobsmacked, mouth hanging open wide.

"How many members does your mother say they have?"

"I think at the last count she said there were about 100 in this area, but she is trying to recruit from all over the country."

"Well I can tell you now, there are thousands in this area, and she is trying to recruit worldwide. I don't know what she is up to, but she is planning something big."

"Dad are you serious? This is Mum we are talking about. All she is bothered about is her cake and hopefully meeting the Prime Minister one day." I looked at him and tried to make sense. After seeing him look so sad recently, it was nice to see him so passionate again about something. It was like he had been waiting to tell me this for a long, long time.

"And that Prime Minister, there's something strange there. Your Mum has always been obsessed with her, even before she was a politician. When she was a famous singer."

"The Prime Minister used to be a famous singer?" I said with disbelief.

"She certainly was. She was in a pop duo called "Two Time" and were relatively successful. Your mother always wanted to go and see them. She wanted to be her best friend. She used to think she could sing like her."

"She still does!" Dad laughed at this and proceeded to tell me all about Two Time and the matching sequin Lycra suits they wore. Dependent on which venue they were playing, it was either baby pink, electric blue or lemon yellow. "The Prime Minister used to dress like that?"

"Look it up on the internet and prepare to be amazed." I did what he said, and I couldn't believe my eyes. There was the Prime Minister, dressed up in these ridiculous clothes. Various pictures of them performing in small, strange looking venues. I thought Dad playing in his band was terrible but looking at "Two Time" made his band looking good."

"So, does Mum know her?"

"Ha, she wishes. She pretends she does and I bet that is why she wants her in Ladies First. Has she not arranged for her to come and do a talk yet?" I gave him a look of realisation.

"She has said she is planning a secret visitor at a time I was meant to be coming to you. But that has changed now."

"Can't you see, it is all planned. She doesn't want me telling you the truth; she is stopping you seeing me and trying to turn you against me." This was a lot to take in. I wasn't quite sure what to believe. While all this was going through my head, I thought now would be a good time to ask Dad about his secret handshake with Mr Byrne.

"Dad, do you remember at parents evening?"

"When I was wearing shorts and sandals?" he replied with a grin.

"Err, yes, that day! Anyway, as Mum and I were walking across the playground, I happened to look back at the class, and I saw you and Mr Byrne doing a crazy handshake. What was that all about?" Suddenly Dad changed, and he seemed to become all secretive.

"You saw that?"

"Yes."

"Er, we were just messing around."

"Come on Dad; you have always told me to tell the truth. You say you know when I'm lying and I can tell now that you are lying to me!" Dad sat there quietly, paused for a second and took a deep breath.

"Ok. This adds a little more to the mystery. I know Mr Byrne. We are friends. We have decided together that we need to make a stand against Ladies First."

"Are you for real?" I shouted. "Are you telling me that all this time you have been having secret meetings with my teacher?"

"It's not like that; it's nothing to do with you. He is keeping an eye on things at school for me."

"Keeping an eye on things, like what? Me? To check I'm behaving."

"No sweetheart, it's nothing like that." He stood up and held my hands. "Mr Byrne is watching one of the teachers at your school. They are a secret member of Ladies First, and they are planning something. I just must make sure that nothing happens to you. You are the most important thing in the world to me, and I have to keep you safe."

"Safe from what? My classmates, the cook? What Dad?"

"Your mother is planning something and trying to involve you in it. Has she told you what is in the lemon drizzle cake?"

"No, why? What has that got to do with anything?"

"She is controlling people with the secret ingredient." I stared at him in disbelief. "I bet she has had lots of meeting at that cocktail bar?"

"Yes, but she just goes there with Carol, has one gin and tonic and comes home. There's no secret organisation or anything. You have taken this all wrong. What is going on?" Dad is embarrassing, but this was taking it to a whole new level. I let go of his hands and sat down on the chair.

My entire world was spinning massively out of control, and I was struggling to stay on board. My mum had told me all these things, and I paid no attention to what she said. I blocked all her negative thoughts about him and ignored them. Now it starts to look like she was right about him. Not only is he embarrassing but it turns out he may be crazy also. The things he said were unbelievable and put my entire relationship and thoughts into question.

Chapter 6 – Separation

I felt so cross with Dad. I felt let down. Not only had he been embarrassing all these years but now he was being plain crazy. Not only did I stop staying over at Dad's but I decided I wasn't going to see him for a while. Well, I say I decided not to see him, but my mum had made the decision. She did lots of things to keep me happy. I was involved in a lot of things to do with Ladies First.

I helped make flyers for her special meeting. The one with the mysterious guest.

I assisted in fruitcake assembly. My mum had decided on the cake of the Prime Minister's head, so not only did she have to bake a cake the size of a lady's head, but also create metal supports for the tiny neck to hold up the gigantic cranium.

I got close to finding the secret recipe for "The Drizzler", but again my mum said I would have to wait until I was an official member of Ladies First.

I sewed together four patches on a patchwork quilt.

I planned and presented a PowerPoint presentation on bees to some members of Ladies First.

I taught my mum how to use the remote control for the DVD player so she could now watch Mamma Mia without me.

At school, things had been a little weird. I did not know whether to talk to Mr Byrne or not. Was Dad telling the truth? Did he really know Mr Byrne? Or if I said something to Mr Byrne would I look an even bigger fool than I felt? I decided, for now, to leave things be.

That did not stop strange things happening. Let me give you some examples of the strange things that started to happen:

We got a new lollipop man outside the school. He looked like a hippie from the 1970's with his long hair and sunglasses. He would make sure we all crossed the road safely but shout things like "Far out," or "Groovy baby." He seemed a bit weird.

Dad always used to say everyone was weird apart from him, but then he'd change his mind and say that he was the weirdo and everyone else was sane. Anyway, this lollipop man told us his name was Tommy, and it was his mission in life to create a haven for all living things to be safe and at one with each other - whether that be children or hedgehogs crossing the road.

One day, before school, Alexa and I were waiting at the crossing, laughing under our breath at Tommy (this wasn't a very nice thing to do I know, but he did act very peculiar) when suddenly a red van came screeching down the road. Alexa and I had set off across the road, and Tommy was in the middle holding up his large lollypop. We could all hear the car accelerating towards the crossing and Tommy pointed at his STOP sign, but the car continued. Alexa and I hurried out of the way as Tommy dived in our direction, guiding us out of harm's way. Looking at the car, I saw the driver as they zoomed past. I know it was at speed, but I could have sworn it was Miss Howell from school except... well except that she had no makeup on.

In school, at lunchtimes, there was a new dinner lady. She was a bit old and had a hearing aid, thick glasses and a blue rinse. For those of you who don't know what a blue rinse is, it is like hair dye for old people with grey hair. It's meant to lighten the hair, but it usually makes it look blue.

Anyway, this new dinner lady was called Doris, and she helped in the kitchen for the first half of dinner, then came on the yard for the second half to make sure everyone behaved themselves. What a seventy-odd-year-old woman would do, I'm not sure, but that was what she was there for.

One day, she had been helping serve the pizzas we were having for dinner. I could see her get trays from the oven full of pizzas. As she took the trays out, I could see below her blue tabard and dress she wore brown wrinkled stockings. It wasn't a pleasant sight. It was if they were two sizes too big for her. Poor Doris. Each time she took a tray out of the oven, she forgot to use the oven glove so would burn her fingers, to which she would give a sharp, high pitched yelp.

I felt sorry for her, but I grinned as it reminded me of Dad when we used to make pizzas at home. He would fry up bacon, onions and mushrooms in a pan, put tomato sauce on a wrap, sprinkle on the cheese and then pile on the toppings. When he took them from the oven, he never used oven gloves either. He'd say that his hands were made of asbestos and that it was no problem.

Doris would then come onto the yard, wearing a headscarf over her precious blue rinse, protecting it from the wind and rain. She would shout and blow her whistle, refereeing the football matches, saying goals were allowed when they shouldn't be and vice versa. Typical of most dinner staff. However, this day was different.

Alexa and I were having a private conversation around the corner, away from everyone else. It was "Secret Corner", and everyone knew that if it was busy, you left people alone there. While there, the ball came bouncing around the corner. One of the boys must have been slightly off target, again. I was about to run over and kick it back when Doris appeared. She did see the two of us as we were hidden right in the corner so what followed was a complete shock.

She waddled up to the ball, but instead of picking it up, she put one foot in front of the ball and the other behind. Then in a sweeping movement, she flicked the ball backwards, over her head and into her hands. To see someone that age doing that was remarkable. As she set off back towards the yard, she skipped into the air, clipped her heels together and waddled back onto the playground. Alexa and I just looked at each other, mouths open wide.

Over the last couple of weeks, in morning sessions, our class had been split up into three groups. One worked with Mr Byrne, one with Mr McKevitt and the third with Miss Howell. This was not ideal - especially as I am in her group.

This involves having to register in Year 6 quickly in five minutes, then spend the rest of the morning (and some afternoons) with her in a tiny room on the other side of the school with her. I hate it. Things were a bit weird with Mr Byrne, but now it felt like he isn't my teacher anymore. SHE is!

Miss Howell isn't bad to us; she just isn't any fun. She makes us work in silence, and she talks in a posh, high pitched voice. It is like someone is continually stood on her toe, or squeezing her fingers in a vice. It's like she is making a point of singling me out in class. Now I am with her every day it feels like she is continually staring and making notes on me, but I can't think why. What's worse is that she has a picture of the Prime Minister in her room. She even makes us watch videos of the Prime Minister from the internet when she is on the news. It's bad enough my mum going on about her at home but to get it at school as well was just ridiculous.

I decided to talk to my friends about what had gone on. I told Holly what my Dad had said about Mr Byrne.

"So, you're telling me your Dad and Mr Byrne are friends?" Holly repeated after I told her.

"That's what he says. I find it a bit hard to believe, don't you?"

"Well, I suppose it's not impossible, but you would have thought your Dad would have told you before," she responded.

"I know, that's what bothers me. It feels like he has been lying to me all this time," I sadly replied. Holly gave me a supportive hug and whispered that it would all be ok. I smiled back at her; hopeful she was right.

After school that day, Holly, Alexa and I set off on our walk home. Now we are in Year 6 our mums decided that we were big enough to walk home together. We all live relatively close to each other and about ten minutes away from school. Our journey home takes the same route and routine every day. Following the walk up the long hill near the school, we go into the local shop. This is an experience in itself.

There are lots of crisps out of date and overpriced cake. The ginger cat called Abe is often found asleep on the shelves among the tins of fruit and soup and the owner, Colin, sits behind the counter staring at the postage stamp TV screen. On the door of the shop, there is a sign that says, "Only one school child at a time", which always makes us laugh as Colin let's all three of us in at once.

"It's only because I know your Dad," he would say to me with a grin on his face. We bought the usual things: a big bag of sweets from the pick and mix, a large bar of chocolate and a bottle of orangeade. When we pay for it, Colin always counts out the change out the coins individually to make sure we get the correct amount. It took a little longer today as there was an old man in front of us in the shop. He kept asking Colin to repeat everything which our shopkeeper found highly amusing.

The old man had a long black coat on with a matching flat cap and a massive grey bushy beard. He seemed to be keeping us in the shop forever. Eventually, he shuffled out of the shop and disappeared towards the park.

When we had finally received our change from Colin, we left the shop and made our way to the park too. We always sat on the swings and ate our horde of goodies, sharing it out of one of Colin's recycled carrier bags. We walked into the play area towards our usual spot. Today, however, someone was sat on our swings - the old man from the shop. There he was, swinging gently backwards and forwards as if a baby on its way to sleep. There were three other free swings, so we decided to continue. As we approached the old man, we could hear a funny noise - snoring.

"He's asleep," Alexa giggled.

"You're joking?" replied Holly.

"Don't laugh," I interrupted. "He must be exhausted. Poor old thing looks like he's walked miles today. Dad says you always have to be nice to old people because one day you'll become one."

"Look at his suit. It looks like it's from a charity shop," Alexa went on. Upon closer inspection, we could see that she was right. Not only did it look old, dirty and shabby but the jacket seemed too big and the trousers too short. It was as if two suits had been put together in a hurry. We sat down and started to swing, listening to the snores of the old man.

"I wonder what he has been up to today?" Holly wondered.

"I bet he's been annoying people in town, getting in the way by being too slow," Alexa butted in.

"Don't say things like that, it's not very nice," I argued. The old man lifted his head.

"Indeed, you are right, my dear. Not very nice at all," came his response. The three of us looked at each other in disbelief. The man started to swing more rapidly in his seat, gradually increasing his height with each swing. "When I was your age, I was always told to be seen and not heard. You, young lady," he ordered in Alexa's direction, "have just been seen but heard for a while. Never judge someone by their appearances or their age, you never know what may happen."

With this, he continued to increase momentum as he got higher and higher. I was a little panicky now for the gentleman's safety. If he should fall, he would seriously hurt himself.

"Please slow down, I don't want you to hurt yourself," I called to him.

"Don't you worry about me, I'm not what I seem." With that, he reached down to his shoes, which did look a little on the large side, and appeared to flick a switch at the back of the heel. The three of us stood in awe as wheels appeared on the bottom of each shoe. "It's not me who needs to be careful. It's you - Trouble!" There was only one person who called me trouble.

"Dad?" I asked cautiously.

"Yippee," came the reply from the old man as he jumped off the swing and landed on the tarmac perfectly on his roller skates. The momentum from his jump sent him hurtling through the playground like a rocket. He landed like a ski jumper and headed towards the climbing frame.

"I think it's my dad," I told the others.

"That is so cool," Alexa replied, "I wish my dad was like that."

"Really?" I blurted out in a shock. Holly just nodded at me. Watching him now, he was ducking and diving out of the way of the climbing frame, the assortment of prams and children, all standing gobsmacked at this old man on wheels.

A young boy with an ice cream sat on the roundabout, spinning gently, unaware of what was approaching. The old man (Dad) zoomed towards the boy and as he approached the roundabout, grabbed the edge and spun around several times. Not only did this increase Dad's speed but made it impossible for the boy to lick his ice cream as the tall whippy mixture began to lean away from him by the force of the spin.

Eventually, the force was too much and the entire top of his ice cream flew off the cone and straight into Dad's face. He then let go of the edge of the roundabout, leaving the boy in tears and headed back in our direction. I could see him now, wearing an ill-fitting suit and with an ice cream face pack on. As he came closer, I was sure he would crash, but after blindly waving his arms around for a while, he wiped his eyes and regained his composure. As he reached us, he lifted his skates, turning them side on, causing him to stop abruptly.

"Hmm, vanilla," he said, licking ice cream from his face. "I'd have preferred strawberry.

Chapter 7 - The Truth

"Dad! What's going on? What are you doing dressed up like that?"

"I needed to see you. I have been keeping an eye on you, very closely. I have been making sure you are safe always. The only time I have been unable to is when you are alone with your mother. I have watched you on your way to school, and I have even kept an eye on you at school." He now pulled me to one side, away from the others.

"You mean you have got Mr Byrne to keep an eye on me?"

"Well he has, but I have been there too," Dad replied with a wicked smile on his face.

"What do you mean?" I answered nervously.

"Let's just say the newest member of staff at St Mary's has always been there for you."

"Dad, are you seriously telling me you have enlisted the help of Doris, an old lady, to keep an eye on me?"

"There's more to Doris than you think. Do you not remember her football skills that day on the playground?" I closed my eyes and thought back to the moment I saw her flicking the ball above her head. That really was quite amazing; to see someone of that age with such skill and athleticism. Then, it gradually dawned on me. How did Dad know about that? There's no way anyone else could have seen that. Dad must have had a secret camera, or seen Doris do it at other times. "Those tights are a bit uncomfortable!"

"What! It was you?" I gasped in amazement.

"Of course it was me," he grinned in response.

"That's crazy," I replied.

"Not as crazy as being a lollipop man too. Far out!"

"You have got to be joking!" I exclaimed. Dad just grinned. He seemed happy with himself that I had not guessed his secret identity and disguises. Holly and Alexa came over to say hello as they now realised the strange old man was Dad. He looked at them suspiciously

You are getting involved in something terrible and I need to protect you."

"What?" I cried, "with these two?"

"No, don't be daft, I mean with your mother," he replied. Suddenly, I received a text message. I hastily looked at my screen to see who it was. In a strange, eerie coincidence, my mother had put "Where are you and who are you with?"

"Who is it?" Dad quizzed me.

"Mum," I answered. Dad started glancing around him. He looked very concerned and worried suddenly.

"She must be watching. My cover has been blown. There will be someone here soon I guarantee. "

"Dad, why would someone come now?"

"Your mother knows I am here. I need to leave now. I will be in contact soon with a plan. In the meantime, ask Holly to get her dad to tell you about 'OTW'." With that, he turned, put on a pair of sunglasses, pulled up his collar like a spy, and skated off, out of the playground.

Holly and Alexa looked at me, and I honestly didn't know what to say to them. I was still shocked by the actions of Dad in his old man suit.

"Can you believe that?" I finally managed to announce to my friends, but as I did a familiar voice called out from the distance.

"Yoo-hoo," came the call. It was Carol. "I thought it was you. I was just passing on my way home from town, and I could see you on the swings. Who was that man you were talking to?"

"It was..." Alexa started.

"...Just an old man!" I interrupted. "He was a bit strange, but he seemed nice enough."

"You shouldn't really talk to strangers, what would your mother say if she knew?" I just looked at her and smiled with the most unconvincing smile. Then it dawned on me. Dad said someone was watching. Within a minute or two of him saying someone was coming, here was Carol, apparently on her way home from town. Coincidence? Possibly. Or was Dad right? Is something going on?

"Thanks for your concern Carol. We're ok. We better be getting off home now. Don't want Mum to worry."

"Oh no dear, imagine that," and with that, she set off out of the playground, shaking her head and mumbling something about being part of the plan under her breath. Once she had disappeared, the three of us huddled together.

"Holly, Dad said something about asking your dad about OTW. Do you know what that is?"

"No, I'm not sure, but we can go and ask him now if you like," she replied.

"Great, let's go."

Holly's dad (Mick) is a mechanic, but he works from home. Dad has known Mick since they were at school. The number of times he told me about the good old days and the things they used to get up to. I miss those stories. Having seen Dad in the playground, it made me miss him even more.

As we arrived at Holly's house, she walked through the front door calling for information.

"Dad, where are you?"

"He's not here, he's gone out," came the reply. Holly's mum came to the top of the stairs. "He just rushed out, covered in oil as usual. What do you need him for?"

"I just wanted to ask him something. "Mum?" Holly began, "do you know what OTW is?"

"OTW? I haven't heard that mentioned in many years. Why do you want to know?"

"My dad mentioned it," I interrupted, trying to look inconspicuous.

"Give me five minutes; I'll have to root out the memories box." Holly's mum turned from the top of the stairs and disappeared into one of the rooms. We all went in the front room and sat down while Holly got us some drinks. After the events we had witnessed, a glass of cloudy lemonade was welcome.

Eventually, Holly's mum returned with a box file in her hands.

"Sorry, it's a bit dusty, though I imagine your dad still has a look through this now and again, reminiscing about the old days." She wiped the box with her hand and blew the dust away. A thick cloud swarmed in the air and hung in the sunshine that flooded in through the window to the outside world. "All the answers you need are in here." She turned to me. "I think you'll find this especially funny. I'll leave you to it." She left the room and went back upstairs to whatever she was doing before. We sat around the box, excited at what we may find inside.

Holly opened the box. Inside was a selection of newspaper clippings, tatty pieces of paper with lists of songs on, photographs and a couple of cassette tapes.

"Look," Alexa yelped, "OTW - Off the Wall."

"Oh no," Holly groaned, "it's my dad's old band. This is so embarrassing." She started flicking through the brown, curled pieces of paper and creased photographs."

"What's this?" Alexa questioned, holding up a cassette tape.

"It's a tape," Holly answered. "People used to listen to music on them many years ago.

"It's the same size as my phone," replied Alexa with a puzzled look on her face. "How many songs can you fit on it?"

"It's not like a phone; it's ninety minutes of music. Prehistoric." Alexa found this hysterical and couldn't stop laughing. I sat quietly taking it all in. Dad had asked me to find out about this for some reason, and I needed to focus on what he was trying to tell me. I flicked through the photographs and couldn't believe what I saw.

"Look at this," I gasped. There in front of me was a picture of four young men. Two with sparkly shirts on, two with red flowery shirts on; long hair was nearly covering their faces, but not long enough to hide their identity.

"That's my dad and yours," Holly laughed.

"I know that, but look at the other two in the picture. Look carefully." Holly and Alexa stared intently at the photograph.

"Is that...?" Alexa gasped.

"Yes, it is. It's Mr Byrne. Look you can recognise his face. I know his hair is a bit longer, but he has the same nose. You can just tell it is him. I didn't know Dad knew him like that."

"And look who the other man is," Holly continued. We all looked. "It's Colin from the shop." Sure enough, there he was. Wearing a very flowery shirt, but looking the same as he does now. The other three looked younger, accurate for twenty or so years ago, but Colin looked old like he does now in the photograph.

What a sight in front of me. I couldn't believe first what they looked like, but secondly that I knew nothing about it. Colin really did look the same as he did every time we went to the shop. He looked much smaller than the others and was holding a pair of drumsticks in his hand.

Mr Byrne had a sparkly blue shirt on, unbuttoned halfway down, showing off a sickly-looking chest wig. Around his neck, he held a red electric guitar, and he was leaning on a microphone stand.

Mick (Holly's dad) looked very different. I had only ever seen him with his bald head, but here he was with long wavy hair, combed neatly into a side parting. He was wearing a similarly sparkly shirt, yet this one was silver and looked a little tight around the stomach. Like Mr Byrne, he was holding a guitar, this time black and leaning on a microphone that looked like Elvis Presley should be using it in the fifties.

Finally, there was Dad. Big bushy hair, no glasses or beard but a face full of spots. I guessed he must have been late teens early twenties. He wore a matching floral shirt to Colin and looked as equally bad. I knew Mick and Dad were the same age, Colin looked prehistoric, and Mr Byrne looked like he was at an after-school club - not as a teacher but as a child.

"What does this mean?" I asked.

"Well, we know that your two dads were in a band together with our teacher and shopkeeper. We know they have known each other a long time, that Colin has always looked old and they have a terrible sense of fashion," Alexa replied sarcastically.

"Why has my dad asked me to ask Holly to ask her dad about it? What does it tell us? What is the point other than laughing at these old pictures?" I scratched my head and continued to flick through the box of secrets.

"Well, I haven't asked my dad yet as he isn't here. I will ask him when he gets back."

"Do you mind if I keep the photograph, I'll bring it back tomorrow," I pleaded with Holly.

"No problem. I will text you later when my dad comes back," Holly replied.

"I need to get back, or Mum will wonder where I have gone," I sighed. With that, I set off on the short journey home. I passed near Dad's house and felt like going and showing him the picture but decided against it. Was someone watching him? Or me?

Mum was sat waiting for me when I got home. She had been a bit preoccupied recently. Her important meeting was coming up this weekend, and she had been running backwards and forwards sorting things out. Well, texting and phoning people and telling them what to do.

"Have you had a nice day?" she asked.

"Yeah fine," I answered calmly. I didn't want her saying anything about Dad. "I saw Carol before, at the playground."

"Yes, she texted me to say she had seen you with your friends. Everything ok?"

"Yes fine." She appeared to be like an interrogator trying to force information from me.

"I need to do some homework. I'll be in my room if you need me."

"Wait one moment please." I panicked. What was coming next? "I want to show you something. Come with me." I started to worry now. Did she know about Dad on the playground? Was I in trouble for that? What had Carol been saying? I cautiously followed her to the kitchen.

"What do you think?" There on the dining table was a cake. A huge cake! It was shaped like the prime minister's head (or meant to be like the prime minister's head). It looked slightly deformed, and the icing on her skin made it look like her face was melting.

"Wow, that's brilliant," I lied.

"Isn't it just," replied Mum rubbing her hands together with joy. I moved closer to inspect further. On the table, as I got closer, I could see numerous photographs of the prime minister. Different shots of her from different angles to help create the 'masterpiece' before me. I also noticed, rather strangely, pictures of Miss Howell.

I decided not to say anything about it as I could sense my mum was watching me. A couple of lemons, some chopped, some whole, lay on the table, along with a test tube and a large syringe. I reached for it and picked it up.

"Is this for the secret ingredient?" I asked harmlessly.

"Put that down at once!" my mum ordered. "Give it to me."

"Sorry, I thought you would just inject the drizzle into the cake," I answered in defence. "I'll just go and do my homework." Now I know syringes are dangerous and shouldn't be played with under any circumstances, but this had lemon drizzle in it. How bad could it be?

I entered my bedroom and fell onto the bed. Why are all the adults acting so weird? I lay there looking at the ceiling when my phone vibrated. It was Holly.

"Dad says - we're putting the band back together for the PM! Does that make any sense?"

"Not at all. Why do they talk in codes?"

"See you tomorrow."

What did it all mean? What was Dad up to? Suddenly there was a yell from downstairs. I ran down quickly to check if my mum was ok.

"What's the matter?" I asked, concerned for her safety.

"I have just had good news and bad news. Something wonderful and something terrible."

"Well, what's the bad news?" I tried to feign interest.

"The band have cancelled for my party on Saturday. I will have to find an alternative, and that will be really tricky at such short notice." I suddenly paid more attention. Was this a coincidence.

"And what's the good news?" I held my breath in anticipation.

"My mystery guest has confirmed her appearance. The Prime Minister is coming to my party on Saturday night. I must ring Carol." She ran off out of the room. Suddenly everything fell into place. I thought back to Holly's text message.

"We're putting the band back together for the PM!"

PM is prime minister and Dad, and his friends are obviously going to be the band who replace the cancelled act.

Chapter 8 - The Plan

There were only a couple of days until my mum's special event, but I needed to contact Dad to find out his plan. This was easier said than done. Texting him was fine, but if everything he said about my mum was true, then the chances were she would intercept any message between us. If I asked her if I could go and see him, this would arouse suspicion with her, and she would then keep me on lockdown. There was also the high possibility that this was all in Dad's head and my mum had done nothing wrong!

The next day at school, Alexa, Holly and I decided to come up with a plan. As it had been dressing up day at school, everyone was in fancy dress. The theme was your favourite book or character from a story. My mum would be there at the end of the day to pick me up, so no chance of me seeing Dad. Since he thought his cover was blown, he no longer appeared as Doris the dinner lady or Tommy the lollipop man. We needed to get his attention and distract my mum for a while so I could talk to him. We needed a costume, but what to pick.

1. A ghost from any ghost story. Very simple - all we needed to do was cut two eye holes in a sheet and put it over our heads. If we got lots of people to do it in class, then my mum would never be able to work out who was who. Perfect. But how would Dad know it was me?

2. A costume that three (or more) people wear but could still work if one person were to sneak out. Something like a Chinese dragon. Same problem though - how would Dad recognise me without my mum spotting my plan?

3. Change costume during the day, so when I come out of school, my mum doesn't recognise me. This I decided was the plan, but what could I dress as so that Dad would recognise me. There was only one choice - Elvis Presley.

Dad was mad on Elvis. For those of you who don't know who Elvis was what have you been doing all your life? Elvis Presley was the king of rock n roll. Dad's idol and role model. The reason for the silly shirts, haircuts and sunglasses. The reason why he always sings that song at karaoke. The reason why he says,

"Thank you very much" in an American accent at least five times a day. Apparently, he died on the toilet eating a burger. Not very hygienic I know, but that was Elvis.

This was my plan. I would go to school in a generic fancy dress costume. This was to be The Cat in The Hat. Face painted, black clothes with tail, red bow tie and oversized hat. The best part was several of my friends said they would wear the same costume to add to the confusion at the end of the school day. This all went to plan. At dinner time, I got changed into my new outfit: a crisp, white jumpsuit decorated with a sequined eagle on the back; a red, silk scarf around my neck; a huge black wig with accompanying sideburns hanging down either side of my face and finally the largest, darkest pair of seventies aviator sunglasses possible.

Wearing this, I would be entirely unrecognisable to my Mum, but Dad would know it was me straight away. When I came into class after dinner, Mr Byrne (dressed as a wizard) gave me a knowing nod and disappeared to make a phone call. When he returned, he called me to the desk.

"I have been in contact with The King," he announced, smiling to himself.

"Ok," I replied, a little unsure.

"Your dad," he explained.

"Oh, right, I get you."

"He will be here after school, in disguise. He says you will know how to recognise him. The secret code is 'You ain't nothing but a hound dog'. Is that ok?"

"Got it. Thanks. Do you know what he is up to?" I quizzed.

"Not yet, but the plan is nearly ready. We have been practising lots of new songs in the band this week."

"Off the Wall?" I shouted.

"Shhh. Yes. But it's top secret," he whispered.

"Ok, got it."

I spent the rest of the afternoon watching the clock, counting the minutes down till home time. Eventually, the bell rang, and we all made our way out of the classroom. As I passed Mr Byrne, he whispered me good luck and out the door I went.

The playground was even more chaotic than the end of a typical day. Every other day, children were running around, excited to be free for several hours before they had to return to school. Today, the playground was full of witches, princesses, and other such characters, along with many cats in hats and one Elvis Presley. I could see my mum, busy talking to other mums, which guaranteed me at least ten minutes while she gossiped about mum things. Holly and Alexa knew what they had to do - make my mum think I was there. I set about looking for Dad. I could not see him straightaway as I knew he was in disguise.

The only adults dressed up were the teachers. Everyone enjoyed this day as it was great fun laughing at the teachers in costume. Miss Gallagher was dressed as a princess, Mr Spencer was dressed as a gnome, Mrs Aspinall had come as Pocahontas, Mr Hargreaves came as the BFG and Mr Sansom was wearing shorts! Miss Howell, however, had her usual fancy dress costume on: her own clothes. She wasn't one for dressing up.

There was one other unusual looking character on the yard, but I didn't know who they were as they were covered in a long white sheet. Two black eye holes and a giant smiley face. That had to be Dad. I cautiously walked over to the white mound and recalled the secret message.

"You ain't nothing but a hound dog."

"Thank you very much," came the reply.

"Dad..."

"Shhh," came the reply. The sheet lifted and a hand appeared. I took it, and I was pulled underneath. There he was. I wrapped my arms around him and gave him a big hug. It felt like ages since I'd had a proper dad hug - the best type of hug. "Hiya trouble. How are you?"

"I'm ok."

"Great costume," he complimented.

"Dad! What's going on?" I interrupted.

"Right, this is the plan. Listen carefully; we don't have long. Your mother's special function is tomorrow night, correct."

"Yes," I replied in anticipation.

"I have made arrangements. She had organised a band - some group called Red Moon Joe, but unfortunately, their lead singer has had an unfortunate accident, and he is unable to sing or play the guitar. Don't worry, I know him, and he has agreed to my plan. He has told your mother of another band that is going to play in their place. That is where Off the Wall come in.

Obviously, we can't use that name as your mother would recognise that so we have changed our name and appearance. This means I will be there to keep an eye on things and, more importantly, you."

"Why, what do you think is going to happen to me?"

"I don't think your mother would purposely harm you, but I do think she wants you in Ladies First. If that happens, you'll be eating lemon drizzle cake, and then that's it."

"Why do you keep going on about the cake Dad?" I was confused. He had mentioned the cake numerous times but never gone into more delicate details.

"There is something in the cake. Have you seen her injecting it with something or adding a secret ingredient?"

"There was a syringe next to the cake the other day. With lots of pictures of the Prime Minister. And… rather strangely… some of Miss Howell."

"Miss Howell. She must be involved somehow. I never trusted her. Their plan involves the Prime Minister and the cake; it must do. Now Miss Howell is involved somehow, and your mother links it all together. I may need your help on the night, but promise me, whatever you do, don't eat any of the cake."

"Ok, I promise," I replied.

"Right, you better go. I can see your mother looking for you." I gave him an extra big hug, and he lifted the sheet. I walked towards my mum, who was currently surrounded by several cats in hats.

"I'm here Mum," I shouted.

"Why are you wearing those ridiculous clothes?" she asked, puzzled as I looked different to half past eight this morning.

"I spilt my drink down myself, and someone had a spare costume," I lied.

"You look very silly. Take off that wig and glasses at once." I did as I was told and followed her off the playground. I turned to look for Dad but he was gone, a lifeless sheet remained on the floor.

Party day arrived, and my mum was even more stressed than usual. We turned up at the venue. Surprise, surprise... it was the cocktail bar. My mum had wanted a fancy hotel or country club, but she said she had got a good deal with Lee. I thought back to the day when I saw a female version of him in the car. Was he trying to run me over? Dad had saved me that day, and I felt safe in the knowledge that he was going to be there today.

The inside of Lee's Bar was very strange. To look at it from the outside, the venue looked like a fancy nightclub with its neon lights and bright signs, and part of it inside matched with a dance floor, spinning lights and mirrored walls. However, the bar area was something completely different. It looked like it belonged in a different decade if not century. The carpet was sticky to walk on, caused by some mystery spillage over the years. There was no pattern or design just a mess of Browns and greens creating the illusion of vomit on the floor.

The wooden bar, ornately decorated with various shapes and motifs, looked tired and lacked love. The walls had been recently refurbished, with paper covered in wine boxes, to give the impression of a fancy wine cellar but it was fooling no one. Rickety, wooden stools sat at the bar, waiting to collapse at a moment's notice. Lesley, one of the barmaids and another member of Ladies First, kept things in order when Lee was not present.

Today, he was nowhere to be seen, much to Carol's displeasure, so Lesley was in charge. I liked her as she gave me free pop and crisps when I came with my mum. However, she did wear a hearing aid, and she was utterly deaf without it. This did cause some confusion at times especially when ordering drinks. People quite often ended up with a strange concoction, rather than their requested beverage. Dad always said that she was just pretending to be deaf. When I asked him why anyone would do that, he always replied,

"She will hear all sorts that people say because people will think she is deaf, but secretly, she is building up information on people, all for the good of Ladies First."

My mum was backwards and forwards all afternoon, barking instructions at different members, but her primary concern now was the band.

"Where on earth are this band?" she muttered in anger. "They said they would be here by now!"

"I'm sure they'll be here if they said they would," I offered in support. "What are they called?" As if by magic, and before my mum could answer, the emergency exit doors by the dance floor flew open. Car lights from outside, and an early evening fog made it appear that they were walking on stage at Wembley Stadium.

"We are Hogweed," came the call from the first person through the door. "Allow myself to introduce ourselves to yourselves." This individual had a huge Afro wig on his head and large black sunglasses. It appeared that he had a beard, but I could tell it had been drawn on, perhaps with felt tip pen. He wore a long flowery kaftan, like an oversized shirt, three sizes too big, and by the unique tone of his voice, I could tell it was Colin. "My name is Boris, and I am the master of percussion, the human metronome." He was twiddling a pair of drumsticks as he made his announcements, feeling very good about himself. He strutted very warily around the stage in a pair of brown leather cowboy boots, shouting yee-haw and pretending to shoot his drumsticks in the air.

"Next, we have on guitar and vocals, direct from a tour of China, Norris!" This person, to the untrained eye, would practically be unrecognisable, but as an expert (and because it was my class teacher) I could recognise it as Mr Byrne. His clothing consisted of sparkling gold pieces of material, strapped in various angles all his body. His chest hair sprouted prominently from a criss-cross of gold, but this was insignificant in comparison to the waterfall of hair, streaming like a torrent from the top of his head. It must have hung four or five-foot long. He too wore sunglasses, but these were star-shaped, matching the seventies theme of his costume.

"Also on guitar and vocals, performing tonight for the first time in nearly twenty years, we have Morris!" This image was hard to explain except for one word. Denim. A white t-shirt, a denim shirt - unbuttoned, a denim jacket, and a pair of denim shorts. All different shades. The strangest thing about this member's appearance was the sensible side parting upon his head.

Although this may not sound strange, it was more the fact that it was Mick (Holly's dad) wearing the hairstyle, something that had been absent from him for years. He seemed so proud to have hair he kept stroking and running his fingers through it, to ensure it was still there.

"Finally," Colin announced, "making her debut performance with Hogweed, on bass guitar, Doris." Her debut performance? Surely not! Out walked Dad, but not wearing his usual band clothes; this time he was wearing high heels, tights and a little black dress. He wore a long red wig and even brighter red lipstick. He appeared to walk a bit uncomfortable, but overall, Dad seemed to enjoy his new clothing range. He waved a little as he entered the room as if a member of royalty.

The band set up and sound checked; the cake was brought in, covered in a pink sheet; all table decorations where positioned, and all Ladies First members were accounted for. It was time for the party to start.

Chapter 9 - The Party

Lee's Bar had never been as busy. Tables were set out on the dancefloor, and the guests had all arrived - all but one. I was very nervous from what Dad had told me. I was waiting for something to happen: something out of the ordinary. The cake was still covered up, and the band were playing a selection of easy listening hits from the last sixty years.

Suddenly, a considerable kerfuffle occurred by the entrance to the club. The guest of honour had arrived. Lots of people were crowding around but mainly members of Ladies First. The Prime Minister was walking into Lee's Bar. She was accompanied by a security detail - two men, both wearing suits and sunglasses, both with earpieces in, talking into their sleeves, like in films with the American president. They never left her side.

Surely Dad's theory couldn't take place because the security was too tight. The Prime

Minister was ushered to her unique table, and my mum was sat next to her discussing no doubt her plans for Ladies First in preparation for the grand cake unveiling.

I decided to leave them to it and went to listen to the band. Dad and his friends were having a great time. They had chosen a wide variety of songs that everyone knew, but Mr Byrne and Mick were changing the words to fit the situation. For example, they were literally singing about the cake being poisonous, but in the style of a seventies disco tune. Or an eighties love ballad about the PM being kidnapped. The problem was no one was listening to them, even though they were quite good.

I sneaked over to where they were playing and managed to grab a quick word with Dad in his dress and high heels.

"How's it going?" he asked.

"Not too bad, but nothing has happened yet," I replied.

"I know, the PM is well guarded so it looks like nothing much can happen. Where is your mother?"

"Talking to the PM," I answered.

"And what about that Miss Howell? You said her picture was there with the cake, that she has been acting strange, where is she now?"

"I'm not sure." I had not seen Miss Howell for a long period of time so decided to set off and find her. "Leave it with me."

I set off around the club, sneaking from pillar to post, inspecting each table to see what was going on. Everything seemed normal, or as usual as could be expected for a Ladies First meeting, but then I spotted her. Miss Howell was applying make to her face, again. She always seemed to be adding makeup to her face. It was like she was wearing a mask. She did not look happy with the application of makeup as the light was not very good for applying foundation. She got up and decided to take a trip to the lady's toilet.

From a distance, I decided to follow. The journey to the bathroom in Lee's Bar was a long one. Up and down flights of stairs, along twisted corridors and through several doors till at last you reached the freezing cold toilets. The final part was down a long corridor so I had no chance of keeping close to Miss Howell as she would see me. I decided to wait in the corridor until she came out and then I would follow her again. No one wants to follow one of their teachers into the toilet.

She seemed to be in there a long, long time and I was about to investigate when I heard the door open again. I peered down the corridor from my hiding place, waiting for Miss Howell to pass, but she did not. The person leaving the toilets was not Miss Howell but the Prime Minister, Mrs Smith.

I was sure the Prime Minister was in the main room with my mum, but she must have decided to go to the toilet when I was talking to Dad. I slipped back into my darkened corner and let the Prime Minister pass. It seemed strange she would visit the bathroom with her protection either side of her, she was not my target tonight. I had to follow Miss Howell. After another five minutes of waiting, I became suspicious. What was taking her so long? I decided to investigate. If Miss Howell were to ask me anything, I had the perfect excuse of needing the toilet. I pushed open the door and went into the bathroom.

The toilets were empty. It appeared there was no one there. I assumed Miss Howell must be in one of the cubicles. I went to each one, slowly and carefully, checking to see which one she was in, but she was not in any of them. This did not make sense. I carefully checked the bathroom for any other exits - none. There was nowhere to hide, and she had not sneaked out past me. I had seen her enter the bathroom but not seen her leave. She must still be in here. The only other person was... Then, I had a sudden horrible feeling inside of me.

Perhaps the person who passed me in the corridor was not the Prime Minister; maybe it was Miss Howell - in disguise as the Prime Minister. I suddenly panicked and was unsure what to do. I decided to re-enter the main room again and see what Dad and my mum were up to. Dad was still playing cheesy tunes in the band, and my mum was still talking to the Prime Minister. I rushed up to Dad.

"Has the PM left that table in the last five or ten minutes?" I quizzed him.

"No, not at all," he replied, the answer I did not want to hear.

"I know what Miss Howell's part in this is. She is disguised as the PM. She looks exactly like her. They must be making a swap."

"Of course, that way they really can take over the country. But they must have some way planned to get rid of the real PM."

"The cake!" we both exclaimed at the same time. I rushed over to the cake and could see Mum and the Prime Minister making their way across for the grand unveiling.

"Mum," I gasped as I got close to her side.

"There you are, I was wondering where you had got to. It's nearly time for your big moment. Time for you to join Ladies First."

"But Mum I know what's going on," I blurted out. She gave me a stern look. One that said do not say anything else or you will be in trouble.

"You are about to join Ladies First, and you will not ruin this night for me, do you understand?"

"But Mum!"

"Do you understand?"

"Is everything ok?" Mrs Smith enquired.

"Oh yes, of course. You know what little children are like. They should be seen and not heard." They both laughed at the comments, though neither seemed convinced of what the other was saying. "Time for your surprise Prime Minister." My mum now picked up a microphone and announced that the special time of the night had come. "As you know I set up this group many years ago now and tonight is the highlight of my time as leader of Ladies First." A large round of applause broke out spontaneously. "Tonight, I am so proud…" Here it comes, I thought to myself. Bigging up the Prime Minister! "Yes, the Prime Minister has joined us tonight, but what makes me prouder still… is that my daughter will join our ranks tonight." An even bigger cheer erupted from the room than before.

I did not expect this. I thought tonight was all about the Prime Minister, but why was Mum doing this now?

"Prime Minister if you please. Could you unveil the cake?" The Prime Minister pulled on the pink cloth and revealed the sizeable, oversized head decorated in very pink icing. If possible, it looked even worse than when I had seen it in Mum's kitchen previously. I think transportation had not worked very well. Everyone applauded politely and gave three cheers for Mum. She seemed very happy with herself.

"Now before we cut up this cake, there are two special pieces I want to give out first. One, of course, to the Prime Minister for visiting our little event tonight. And the second to my daughter as a sign of reaching the age to become a fully-fledged member of Ladies First." She produced two plates with a perfect piece of The Drizzler on it. The PM's eyes nearly popped out of her head.

"Thank you very much," she replied and proceeded to take huge bites out of the cake as quickly as possible.

"Come on dear, your turn now," Mum cajoled me. I remembered what Dad had said. I promised him I would not eat any of the cake.

"Thanks Mum but I'm a bit full at the moment," I replied.

"Eat the cake," she barked at me.

"I'd rather not if that's ok."

"Eat it. NOW!"

"No!" A voice called out across the room and caused a hush to fall over everyone there. It was Dad, in his short black dress and high heels. "Don't eat that cake; it's poisoned."

"It's wha…" started the Prime Minister before collapsing to the floor. Her security guards did not know what to do, and a crowd gathered around the Prime Minister. Suddenly the Prime Minister was back on her feet and escorted out of the room by the two security men.

"You fool," Mum shouted. "Look at you, what a pathetic human being you are."

"At least I'm not trying to poison our child," Dad responded.

"You have no idea," Mum bellowed back at him. "Ladies… grab him."

At this point, I was hurried out of the room by Carol; Dad, along with the rest of the band, were also guided from the main room.

"Our plan has worked," Mum announced, her eyes lit up with delight. "We have managed to swap the PM with Miss Howell. We now have the leader of the country as a member of Ladies First."

"Where is the real Prime Minister?" I asked.

"She is still on the floor under the cake table where she collapsed. You see, Miss Howell was told to be ready, she got changed and into position. As soon as the cake was eaten, places were swapped, and we could carry on as if nothing else had happened."

"But why do you want me to eat the cake?" I responded, concerned for my safety.

"Because you need to change your way of thinking, and get away from that silly man."

"But Mum, he has been telling the truth all along."

"He is a fool," Mum bellowed at me. "Nothing he has ever done in his life has ever amounted to much. He is a complete waste of space. A little piece of cake and the secret ingredient would help you start to believe that. Just try and you will see." I could not believe what I was hearing. Not only had Dad been telling me the truth all along, but now Mum wanted to poison me to forget all this had happened. All those times she had prevented me from seeing him and he was right all along. I could not forgive her for this. I had to help him escape.

"Come quickly, the Prime Minister is waking up," a voice called from the doorway.

"Keep an eye on her," Mum said about me. "She's still got some cake to eat." All the ladies left the room to return to the principal place

101

where the cake and Prime Minister where. All apart from one.

This lady was unfamiliar. I knew most of my Mum's friends but this one was unknown. It was possible she had just turned up for the meeting but why leave a stranger in charge of the daughter of the leader of Ladies First? This lady had long black hair, draped over her face, so I could not get a clear look at her face. She wore a slim fitting little black dress, black tights and somewhat cumbersome black high heeled shoes. The only other thing that made her stand out was her arms. They were hairy; very hairy. She looked like a slim lady but someone had changed the arms of a gorilla. I did not know what to do so desperate times call for drastic measures.

"Listen, I don't know who you are but my Mum has lost the plot. This might sound daft but she has poisoned the Prime Minister and is trying to poison me. She has also taken my Dad and his friends' captive. Is there anything you can do to help?"

For a second, she just stood there, her face still covered. However, the actions that followed next made me smile. The lady in black flicked back her hair and underneath; there was a heavily made-up face: orange cheeks, blue eyeshadow and scarlet red lipstick. All of this was applied in a particularly unfashionable way, but after seeing the face, it was clear why. In a deep voice, the reply came.

"Don't you think I don't know that?" It was Lee.

Chapter 10 - My Dad

I stood there: initially amazed, then slightly confused, then concerned, but finally happy. Lee explained.

"Right, believe it or not, I have been helping your Dad. I volunteered to go deep undercover in Women's First. I didn't quite realise that it would involve a change in fashion but I have finally mastered high heels and I think I suit a pair of tights very well." I grinned. It seemed Dad knew everyone and had a plan for all scenarios. I suddenly wondered about Lee's love interest.

"What about Carol? I think she really likes you Lee."

"Oh, don't worry about her. I'll buy her a bunch of flowers and a box of chocolates and she'll be right as rain." I sat there thinking of her reaction. She would potentially be distraught, but Lee was right, a few presents and she would soon be back on side. "What's the plan?"

"Well, we need to release your dad and his friends, we then need to stop the switch of the PM and sort out these ladies."

"And how do we do that?"

"Follow me." We set off down a long, winding corridor, and I followed, as requested, as Lee teetered and tottered upon his four-inch heels. For someone who had claimed to have mastered high heels, he was not doing a very good job. He approached two other ladies standing outside what appeared to be dressing rooms, both with large handbags over their arms. I could see he was about to address the ladies, but I was curious as to what voice would come out of his mouth. I expected a falsetto, high pitched shrill shriek to fool the heavily armed guards, holding their rapid-fire purses. I could not be further from the truth.

"I've brought our leader's daughter down here. She has to verify the identity of the other band members." He spoke in a deep low-pitched voice that anyone would surely guess belonged to a man. I was starting to panic. The game was up.

"Ok," spoke the first guard, amazingly in a similar low-pitched voice. There was nothing out of the ordinary here.

"You have five minutes," continued the second burly voiced guard, again, fitting in perfectly to the conversation. The first guard leaned and opened the pink door, emblazoned with a star and the label Dressing Room 1. I was ushered in by Lee to a pitch-black room.

"Prepare to talk boys, or we will start the torture again." The door closed behind us as an array of bulbs exploded into life around the long mirror, above a dressing table. In front of it, looking very forlorn and dejected, sat the three other band members: Colin, Mr Byrne and Mick. They were all gagged with thick black tape over their mouths and missing elements of their costumes.

Colin was upset about his lack of cowboy boots that had boosted his height by several

105

centimetres. Mr Byrne appeared upset about the lack of sunglasses, as he no longer felt like a rock star. Mick was distraught at the lack of hair upon his head for the wig he had worn before was now gone and red raw patches remained upon his flesh where the hairpiece had been removed with some considerable force.

The tape was pulled hastily and roughly from the band member's mouths.

"Where's Dad?" I asked once they had stopped wincing from the pain of tape removal.

"Carol took him," replied Mr Byrne. Lee and I were cutting through the tape that held the men's hands tightly behind their backs. "We need to get him out."

"Wait," I shouted, "we will. But it's going to be hard to rescue him from Carol. You three need to try and free the PM and then get her and yourselves away from here."

"Agreed," Lee nodded. "We will find him and meet you guys later." The three remaining band members took positions either side of the door and as Lee and I were about to leave the room, the lights were turned off. The door swung open. "These men are useless," Lee complained to the two guards. "They have requested to speak to you." We both passed through the doorway and turned to see the two ladies enter the room. The door slammed behind them and a loud ruckus could be heard from the room. A couple of minutes followed and Mick could be heard shouting.

"Turn on the lights." Next, all that could be heard was laughter. Lee returned to the door and opened it. I could see him shaking his head as he turned around to me. Looking in, I could see why there was laughter in the room. Upon the three chairs that the men had been tied and gagged, there now sat the two female guards, similarly bound and muted, but somehow, in the middle of them, sat Colin, bound and gagged as he was before. Mick and Mr Byrne just laughed. Lee spoke quietly to them and they proceeded to untie their mistaken victim.

"Our turn," Lee announced. "But first I need to unleash the secret weapon. Have you got a baby wipe?" He disappeared into his office, which was situated a few doors down from the dressing room. Unsure what was happening inside, I began to wonder about Dad and his safety, and what exactly I would say to my mother the next time I saw her. This did not go on for long.

Lee suddenly burst through the door, ready for action. Gone were the tights, heels and makeup. Now, it was the turn of the beard, flat cap and slicked back hair.

"If we're going to get past Carol, we are going to need some charm."

"Now that sounds like a plan," I replied. "But where will Dad be?" I asked.

"I bet he is locked in the cellar." Sure enough, as we approached the cellar, Carol could be seen outside the cellar door. There was no secretive behaviour or subtle actions: Lee just walked straight up to Carol, grabbed her and in a swooning manner, swept her off her feet as he kissed her. She appeared to literally turn into a piece of ice in his hands and just melt. As he was busy smooching her, He waved his hand behind his back, gesturing me through the cellar door. I walked in through the stone archway, down three small flights of stairs and there he was, locked in a metal cage.

"What are you doing here?" he shouted from his jail cell.

"I've come for you. Lee is up there with Carol, keeping her occupied."

"Really?" came Dad's response. "I always thought there was something going on between those two. Anyway, you should have got away from here. Far away. It's not safe. You heard what your mother said."

"She's crazy. You were right all along. I cannot believe this. What's going to happen?"

"Well," Dad responded with a big sigh, "you can come and live with me. Once I'm out of this cage. Can you find something to open this lock?" I held up my hand.

"You mean this?" I answered sarcastically, dropping a key from my hidden palm.

"Brilliant. Get this door open and let's go home."

"Not so fast," a familiar, shrill voice sounded from the darkness. It was my mother.

She appeared from behind some barrels of beer and boxes of cheese and onion crisps, like an evil gang leader lurking in the shadows. Her positive, optimistic feeling of the evening before had now disappeared and a familiar, hard-faced look was apparent. She walked towards the cage in which Dad was enclosed.

"Well, you have managed to ruin my plans tonight. You have managed to bumble your way through the evening as you do through life daily. If you had an ounce of intelligence, you'd have never got involved in this." Dad just stood there, looking despondent and disillusioned

"Dad, do something?" I screamed at him, but still nothing. He just looked like he had given up and could not be bothered anymore. Everything he had worked out, the plans he had put into place, and now he was reduced to being locked in Lee's cellar.

"No, my dear, now you will see what a pathetic little man he is. All his friends have left him, and very soon, you and I shall leave him here, and you will take your rightful place in Ladies First."

"I won't," I retaliated.

"Do as your mother says," Dad replied from his cell.

"Why?" I questioned with tears in my eyes.

"Because, it is for the best," and with that, he turned his back to face the rear of the cellar.

"But Dad…"

"Go with your mother." My mother held out her hand and beckoned me towards her. I reluctantly took her hand, and she led me towards the stairs at the exit of the cellar. As we approached the stairs, there was a familiar view on the bottom step. There stood Carol, no Lee in sight, only clutching a box of cheese and onion crisps.

"Ah Carol, at last. Where have you been? Why are you holding that box? I know you like crisps, but that is ridiculous. There has been enough stupidity and foolishness tonight without you being involved. Out of my way, I need to get this child of mine home and dealt with." My mum made her way towards the bottom step, but Carol would not move. "Carol? What are you doing? Get out of my way?"

"No," came the reply.

"I beg your pardon; do you realise what you are saying? Get out of my way now!"

"And I said no," responded the rejuvenated Carol. "For too long have I taken orders from you and for what? Nothing. Look what we have now? We will just go back and make another plan to try and take over the world, but I don't want that anymore."

"And what," replied my mother, "do you want?"

I want a normal life."

"Ha-ha, a normal life? Who with?"

"With him," Dad answered. I spun around to see Dad and Lee now both in the metal cage.

"Him? Lee?" my mother retorted with a loud scoff. "He has managed to lock himself in the cage also. Hardly catch of the year Carol."

"But that is where you are wrong," Carol replied. "My man Lee has been up to the bar and travelled down the hatch behind the bar to reach the locked cell. But he has a key in his hand and whilst you have been busy moaning and complaining about your failed plan; he has opened the gate to the cage." Following this, as if by magic, the cage door swung open and out walked Lee and Dad, still dressed in his dress and high heels, now wigless and with smudged makeup.

"And what exactly do you think you can do now?" challenged my mother. A smug look coming over her face, as if nothing Lee or Dad could do would hurt her.

"This!" shouted Carol as she picked up the box of crisps and, using the circular opening at the end of the box, thrust it over my mum's head. Due to the narrowness of the opening, it was unable to be removed, and Mum was wandering around blindly, with muffled screams emerging from inside the box. The more she struggled with removing it, the quicker and more erratic she moved until she ran full speed into a wall, knocking herself out. I turned and ran to Dad and hugged him tightly.

"Are you ok?" he asked brushing the hair from my eyes.

"I am now," I sighed with relief.

"Sorry this took so long, I had to stall your mother while I was waiting for Lee to come with the key."

"You had all this planned?" I gasped. I turned to see Lee and Carol hug in a romantic embrace. Carol, swooning to his endless charms, gazed longingly into Lee's eyes as he reversed his cap and kissed Carol.

"Of course. And if Lee hadn't been able to help, I had a backup plan, but that would take a little longer to work."

"What do you mean?" I quizzed my Dad, wondering what this plan could be.

"It's a little embarrassing!" Dad replied, sighing under his breath. I could hear the door at the top of the stairs swing open. I expected a mad rush of Dad's friends or maybe even the police but no, only anticipation of who may come around the corner.

"Did someone say embarrassing?" The instantly recognisable frame, knitted jumper, smart blazer and bald head could only mean one thing.

"Grandpap!!" I shouted. Dad laughed at the sight of his father.

"Now that is one embarrassing Dad!"

Epilogue

News Flash

Following the incidents several months ago involving our excellent Prime Minister, Mrs Smith has very graciously decided to release some members of Ladies First who were involved in a kidnap attempt. These significant members have since disappeared, and when the Prime Minister was questioned about this at a recent afternoon tea session, she merely responded

"At the time, it seemed like a good idea. But never mind about that, pass me more of that lemon drizzle cake!"

More titles by Chris Allton

www.chrisallton.co.uk